The Puppy Who Ran Away

The Puppy Who Ran Away

by Holly Webb

Illustrated by Sophy Williams

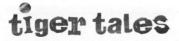

tiger tales

For Alice

tiger tales

5 River Road, Suite 128, Wilton, CT 06897
Published in the United States 2023
Originally published in Great Britain 2021
by the Little Tiger Group
Text copyright © 2021 Holly Webb
Illustrations copyright © 2021 Sophy Williams
ISBN-13: 978-1-6643-4043-5
ISBN-10: 1-6643-4043-2
Printed in China
STP/3800/0483/0822

www.tigertalesbooks.com

Contents

Chapter One
A Strange Day

Isabella picked at her breakfast. She wasn't really hungry, but she knew that Grandma and Grandpa were keeping an eye on her. She took a bite of toast to make them feel better.

Grandpa smoothed her hair. "You're so quiet."

Isabella swallowed hard, trying to get the mouthful of toast to go down her throat. She smiled at Grandpa, but it came out a little wrong.

Grandma looked at her anxiously. "It's going to be all right, Isabella. I know it's a strange day, but it'll be so nice to see your mom again, won't it?"

Isabella nodded, since she couldn't get any words to come out around the dry toast. Grandma was right—she had missed Mom so much over the last two weeks, and she was desperate to see her. She'd loved being at Grandma and Grandpa's while Mom was on her honeymoon in Greece, but she'd never been away from Mom for so long, and she wanted to go home.

The problem was, she wasn't going home. Not really.

She was going to Mike's house. It

was supposed to be Mom's house and her house now, too, but it just wasn't. It belonged to Mike and his son, Sam. Mom had explained that it made sense for them all to live there together after the wedding, because Mike's house was bigger than theirs. There was a beautiful bedroom that Isabella could have, and Mom had promised she could paint it any colors she liked. Isabella liked her old bedroom. It was a little grubby and small, but she didn't care. It was hers.

She was trying *so hard* to be happy, because her mom was happy. Mom kept smiling all the time, and she sang while she was cooking, and when she was on the phone with Mike, she was always laughing. Isabella really liked Mike, too. He was funny and he told silly jokes, silly enough to make Isabella cry with laughter sometimes…. It was just a lot—suddenly having a stepdad and a stepbrother and a new house and a new bedroom.

"Finish your breakfast, Isabella," Grandpa said. "You don't have long before your mom gets here to take you to Mike's house … I mean, your house…."

Grandma gave him a look and then turned to Isabella. "She said she'd be here about nine. Do you have everything packed?"

"Yes," Isabella mumbled at last. "I put my things in the hallway." She'd only had a small bag of clothes and her school things with her at Grandma and Grandpa's—everything else from her bedroom had already been moved.

On Monday, she'd be going to school from the new house, instead of walking with Grandma and Grandpa. They often took her to school when Mom was on a shift at the nursing home, and of course they'd taken her every day while Mom and Mike were away.

That was one good thing about moving—Mike and Sam's house was close to school, and her best friend, Beatrice, lived next door. Her mom and Beatrice's mom had agreed that they were old enough to walk to school together now on their own.

When Isabella and Beatrice had suggested it, Mike had told their moms that Sam used to walk to school on his own in fourth grade. Sam was in sixth grade now, so he went to the middle school, which was in the other direction. Isabella had sort of known him even before his dad started dating her mom, since their school wasn't very big. She'd never imagined she'd end up sharing a house with him, though. It was going to be so strange, after it had been just her and Mom for so long.

Isabella froze in her seat as she heard

a car pull up. A moment later, the doorbell rang. Isabella forgot all about the weirdness, almost tipping over her chair as she rushed to answer the door.

Mom swept Isabella up into a huge hug as soon as the door opened. "Oh, I've missed you!" she said, laughing into Isabella's curly hair.

"Me, too! Did you have a good time?"

"It was wonderful. We'll have to go back there one day, all of us."

Isabella pressed her face into Mom's shoulder. That was another weird thing—family vacations were going to be the four of them now.

"So, ready to go to the house?" Mom asked gently.

"Yes," Isabella whispered. "I'll get my stuff."

Grandpa was already picking up her bags and passing them to Mike, while Grandma kissed her good-bye.

"Sam's looking forward to seeing you," Mike said as they got in the car, but Isabella thought he was probably just being polite. Mike and Mom had arranged several outings for the new family, so she and Sam could get to know each other before the wedding, but she hadn't seen him while her mom

and Mike were in Greece. He'd stayed
at his house—*their* house, she had to try
and think of it as their house—while
his dad was away. His nana had come to
stay and take care of him.

"Oh, and you can meet Honey!"
Mom said enthusiastically. "Sam's puppy
… remember I told you about her?
She's adorable." She turned around to
smile at Isabella, and Isabella nodded.

Mom had told her that Mike and
Sam had adopted a puppy from the
animal rescue center about a month ago.
Isabella hadn't had a chance to meet her
yet, but she was really looking forward
to it. She loved dogs, but she had never
had one. Mom had been worried about
leaving a dog alone at home when she
was at work. Living at Mike and Sam's

house was going to be weird, but Isabella kept on telling herself, *At least now I get a dog....*

"I'll bet she'll look much bigger now," Mike said. "She was only about eight weeks old when we brought her home from the rescue center. I've got a feeling she's going to be huge when she's fully grown."

"Mom said Honey was a spaniel. Or mostly a spaniel?" Isabella said, leaning forward a little.

"The rescue wasn't absolutely sure, but they think a little spaniel and maybe some golden retriever. She's a beautiful golden brown color."

"And she has beautiful fluffy ears," Mom put in. "But the most important thing is that she's so friendly and sweet!"

"We could all go for a walk with her this afternoon," Mike suggested. "Here we are. Oh, there's my mom watching for us." He parked the car and waved to a lady standing by the window at the front of the house.

Isabella slowly got out of the car, watching the front door open. Sam's nana was waving at them, but Isabella didn't really know what to do. She didn't feel like she could just walk into the house. She went around to the trunk and picked up her bags.

"It's okay," Mom said, coming to stand next to her. She put an arm around Isabella's shoulders. "I know it feels strange. Take it slowly, all right?"

Isabella nodded gratefully and then laughed out loud. Sam had suddenly appeared at the door, with his arms full of fluffy golden dog. Honey was wriggling and squirming and squeaking with excitement—it looked like Sam was having a hard time holding on to her.

Mom laughed, too. "I told you she was pretty, didn't I? Wow, she really has grown…." She shepherded Isabella along the gravel driveway to the house, and Isabella tried to smile and look happy to be there. Actually, it was a lot easier than she'd thought it would be, since there was Honey acting as though meeting her was the most amazing thing that had ever happened. The puppy was leaning out of Sam's arms, trying to reach Isabella to lick her, and her tail was wagging so fast it was thumping against Sam's hoodie.

"Hey…," Sam said. He seemed a little embarrassed, but he made Honey wave a soft golden paw at Isabella. "This is Honey. Is it okay if I put her down? You're not scared of her, are you? I don't think I can hold her much longer."

Isabella shook her head. "I'm not scared. I love dogs."

"Oh, good." Sam looked relieved. "Your mom said you did, but I was still worried. We're trying to train her not to jump up, but she gets bouncy around new people." He backed into the hall to get out of the way of the bags and crouched on the floor with Honey. "Shh, calm down…."

Isabella watched them doubtfully. Was it okay to get on the floor with Honey, too? She didn't want to go too fast and frighten the puppy. Then Honey squirmed out of Sam's arms at last and lay across Isabella's sneakers, wriggling around and waving her paws in the air. She gazed up at Isabella with huge, dark eyes and whined hopefully.

Sam laughed. "She likes you!"

Isabella couldn't stop the smile spreading over her face. Honey was so soft and warm and wriggly on her feet. She kneeled down and let Honey lick her hands and climb into her lap. Maybe everything was going to be all right.

Honey nuzzled her nose under the girl's chin with little whines of pleasure. A new person! And this girl was scratching her ears now, her favorite spot. Honey sighed happily and slumped into Isabella's lap.

"She *definitely* likes you," Sam said, sounding a little surprised, and Honey looked up at him, hoping that he'd crouch down and fuss over her, too. He stayed standing, though, watching as the girl rubbed Honey's ears, and whispered how beautiful she was. Honey gave the girl one last lick on her chin and hopped out of her lap, trotting over to lean against Sam's legs instead.

Chapter Two
A Walk in the Woods

"Sam, why don't you take Isabella with you to walk Honey?" Mike suggested, and Isabella looked around hopefully. She'd been doing her math homework at the kitchen table. Over the last couple of weeks of living at the new house, she'd discovered that Mike was really helpful with math. He was emptying the dishwasher, but he kept stopping to lean over her shoulder and point out where she'd gotten mixed up.

"She's doing her homework," Sam said. Honey was bouncing around his feet—she obviously knew exactly what the leash in his hand meant.

"I'm almost finished. I'm on the last one!" Isabella said, scribbling frantically. "Done!"

She looked up at Sam, and she was almost sure he sighed. She didn't really mind, though. He'd been okay with suddenly having her around all the time, and Isabella knew it must be as strange for him as it was for her. Every so often Sam wandered into the kitchen or the living room and looked totally shocked to find her there, almost as if he'd forgotten about her for a moment. It was probably good that they were at different schools, she thought, so they weren't on top of each other the whole time.

Was it too much, wanting to go for a walk with them? Honey was definitely Sam's dog. Isabella got to pet her and fuss over her, but Sam was the one who fed her, and he was in charge of her walks. Isabella glanced at him sideways, trying to see if he was annoyed, but he looked okay. They had been on a few family dog walks in the couple of weeks since she'd moved in, but Isabella hadn't been out with just Sam and Honey yet. She was a little jealous that Sam was allowed to go out on his own, but he was two years older than she was, and he had his own phone in case he got into trouble.

She dashed into the hallway to put on her sneakers, and Honey followed her. The puppy was whining with excitement and trying hard to lick Isabella's face as she sat on the bottom step tying her laces.

"Ughh!" Isabella giggled. "I'll never be ready if you keep doing that. Get off my shoelaces, silly." She put her arm around Honey and then rubbed her cheek against the little dog's soft ears.

"Ready?" Sam asked.

Isabella nodded. "Where are we going? The park?" All four of them had been to walk Honey in the park a few times now. Honey loved watching the ducks on the lake.

"Me and Honey usually go to the woods. Pine Grove—there's a shortcut around the corner."

Isabella stared at him blankly, and Sam looked surprised. "You've never been there? It's great. It's small, but there are a bunch of paths and they cross over each other, so it feels bigger. There's a stream, too. Dad used to take me there to build forts and stuff." Sam

leaned down to clip on Honey's leash.
"Come on, Honey. Walk!"

Isabella followed them out of the
front door, admiring the way Sam
coaxed Honey along. The puppy was
enthusiastic about walking, but she
wanted to stop and sniff every stone,
every lamppost, every patch of weeds.
It took them a good ten minutes to
get to the end of the street. Sam kept
pretending to sigh and roll his eyes,
making Isabella laugh. Then he led
them along a little alley with tall fences
either side.

"Oh! You can see these trees from
the yard!" Isabella said, spotting a sign
at the end of the alley that said Pine
Grove.

"Yeah, we're lucky it's so close.

Honey, look! Trees! Come on!"

Honey yapped excitedly and managed to get about thirty feet down the alley without stopping to sniff anything, which was a record.

The woods had a big patch of grass in front that was ankle-deep on Sam and Isabella, but Honey was practically up to her nose. She went galloping through the grass with her ears flying, doing a huge bouncing leap every few steps so she could see where she was going.

"Can we let her off the leash?" Isabella asked, jogging along next to Honey and Sam.

Sam shook his head. "Not yet. Maybe when she's been to more training classes. She's still not very good at coming back when she's

called." He looked around as if he
thought someone might be listening
and then said, "Don't tell Dad, but
she slipped out of the front door once
while he was away. Nana answered the
door for the mail carrier, and Honey
went right between her feet. She
was halfway down the street before I
caught up with her." He shuddered,
and Isabella frowned worriedly.

"Wow, that must have been scary."

"Yeah. So I'm keeping the leash
on for now." He gave Isabella a
considering look. "But you can hold it
if you like."

Isabella stared up at him in surprise.
She'd been hoping forever to be
allowed to walk Honey herself, but
she hadn't been brave enough to ask.

Honey was Sam's dog, and she didn't want to get in the way. "Really? Yes, please! I'll be so careful!"

Sam handed over the leash. "Just don't let her pull it out of your hand. She's little, but she can pull hard if she gets excited."

Isabella nodded. She gripped the leash so tightly that her knuckles started to turn white, but it was so amazing, feeling Honey dance and tug at the end of it. Isabella felt scared and happy and responsible all at the same time.

"Come on, I'll show you the stream."

Sam led them through the gate into the woods and Isabella looked around, surprised at how shady and cool it was under the trees. She sniffed at the strange woody smell—trees and damp earth. Sam was right—they were so lucky to have a place like this so close. There were even a few daisies on the slope that they were passing now. Honey buried her nose in the flowers and sneezed.

"Look." Sam stopped, pointing to a little stream trickling along below them. "It's not very big, but Honey loves splashing in it." The puppy was peering down at the water and wagging her tail wildly. She pulled a little, as if she were planning to jump in, but Sam gave Isabella's bright white sneakers a worried look and put his hand on the leash. "Maybe not in those. We can do it another day."

Isabella smiled. Another day. That meant another walk.

Honey yawned and stretched, then looked around the kitchen. It was definitely breakfast time, she knew. Sam would be coming to feed her soon, and then he'd get his own breakfast and talk to her while she ate her biscuits. Honey scrambled out of her basket—it was still a little too big for her—and trotted over to scratch at the kitchen door.

Nothing. She tried again, a little louder, and this time, she did hear footsteps—but it didn't sound like Sam. These footsteps were lighter. Honey gave a slow, puzzled wag of her tail and sat down to watch the door.

It opened just a crack, and someone peered into the kitchen. Honey thumped her tail on the floor and panted happily at Isabella.

"Hey…. Are you hungry? Is that why you were scratching? I came down to watch TV, but I don't think Sam's up yet." Isabella slipped into the kitchen.

Honey closed her eyes blissfully as Isabella scratched behind her ears. Then she got up and padded over to look meaningfully at her empty food bowl.

Isabella glanced back at the kitchen door uncertainly and nibbled her thumbnail. Honey watched the girl

with her head to one side. What was
the matter? Why did she look so
worried?

Then at last, Isabella went to the
cupboard where Honey knew her
food was kept. Honey sped up her
tail wagging and gave a little bark of
encouragement. She watched eagerly
as Isabella pulled the bag of puppy
food out of the cupboard and reached
inside it for the measuring cup.

"Hey! What are you doing?"

Honey whirled around, her ears
twitching in confusion, and Isabella
jumped, nearly spilling the bag of food.
Sam was standing by the door in his
pajamas. Honey wanted to race to him
so he could make a fuss of her the way
he always did when he came down

in the morning. But Sam's voice was different—sharp and strange. He came stomping across the kitchen toward her and Isabella, and Honey thought he even smelled different. She whined anxiously and backed away a little as he stood over Isabella. This wasn't her Sam....

"You don't feed her!" Sam snapped. "She's my dog!"

"I'm sorry…," Isabella faltered. "She was whining. I thought she was hungry…."

"I was coming. Just leave her alone!"

"Stop shouting," Isabella said, folding her arms. "I was only trying to help. Look, you're scaring her!"

He glared at her. "I didn't do anything! You're the one stealing my dog."

Honey watched miserably as Isabella dashed out of the kitchen, and Sam grabbed the bag of food and the measuring cup. She didn't understand what had just happened, but she hated the hot, fizzing anger that was filling the room. The biscuits rattled sharply into her metal bowl, but somehow, Honey wasn't hungry anymore.

Chapter Three
Sam's Apology

Isabella didn't tell Mom or Mike what Sam had said to her that morning. She didn't want anyone else to know. She just buried it down deep and tried to stay out of her stepbrother's way. But Mom and Mike always encouraged them to spend time together on the weekend, so it was tricky. Isabella had to keep pretending that she had extra

homework so she could stay in her
room without anyone asking her why.
She was pretty sure that Mom was
giving her worried looks, but she didn't
say anything.

Isabella was trying to avoid Honey,
too, and she hated it. She didn't want
Sam to get upset with her again, and
she supposed he was a little bit right.
Honey *was* his dog, even if she had
only been trying to help. If Honey
had been hers, she might have been
upset, too. Although she was sure she
wouldn't have been so mean about it.

Honey didn't seem to realize that
Isabella was trying to stay away from
her. Isabella supposed it wouldn't
make much sense to a puppy. Only the
day before, they'd been on that walk

together to the woods, and Sam had let
her hold Honey's leash.

On Monday before school, Honey
scurried between Sam and Isabella as
usual, watching eagerly for dropped
toast crusts. Isabella tried not to pay
any attention to her, but how was
she supposed to ignore those gentle
nudges from Honey's damp nose? The
nudges were getting harder and harder,
and then Honey put her paws up on
Isabella's knee and licked her arm
hopefully.

Isabella darted a worried glance
at Sam, but she didn't think he'd
noticed. He was gobbling his breakfast
and trying to message someone on
his phone at the same time. Isabella
slipped Honey the corner of her piece

of toast and gently pushed the puppy back down. She wanted to rub Honey's ears and tell her she was beautiful, but she knew she'd better not, just in case.

Isabella swallowed a sigh. How was she supposed to live in the same house as a beautiful puppy and not pay her any attention?

Isabella was quiet all day at school, trying to figure out what she was going to do about Honey and Sam.

"Why are you walking so slowly?" Beatrice asked as they came around the corner onto their street. "You've hardly said anything all day. What's the matter?"

Isabella sighed. She still hadn't told

anyone about her fight with Sam the day before, but maybe it would help to talk about it. "You have to promise not to tell your mom, because she'd tell mine," she warned.

Beatrice nodded. "Okay."

"It sounds so silly…," Isabella said. "I got up early yesterday, earlier than anyone else. I thought I'd go and watch TV for a while. But when I went downstairs Honey was awake, and she was scratching at the kitchen door, so I went to say hello. And then she was hungry. She was acting like she was starved! So … I got her food out." She heaved another huge sigh. "That's when Sam walked in and started shouting at me. He said I was trying to steal her!"

"Oh, that's not fair! You were only

trying to help!"

Isabella shrugged. "Yeah. But I keep thinking, if it was the other way around, I'd probably feel the same…. He has to share everything now. His house. His dad." She sniffed. "But he didn't have to shout at me!"

"Ignore him!" Beatrice said. "He'll get used to it. Anyway, if he's mean, you can come over to my house, okay?"

Isabella nodded and sniffed again. Beatrice had made her feel a little better, but she still had to share a house with Sam—and Honey.

Honey lifted her head from her basket. Was that the door? She loved it when Sam and Isabella got home from school. She yelped delightedly and raced down the hallway. Mike was home during the day, but he was always too busy to play with Honey for long. He took her for a walk at lunchtime, but for the rest of the day, Honey snoozed in her basket, chewed her toys, and wandered around the backyard.

But now Isabella was home! She bounced next to the front door until Mike came to open it, and then she flung herself at Isabella, desperate for love and ear rubs. Isabella shut the door quickly, which was a shame, because

Honey would have liked to go out and explore, but then Isabella crouched next to her. She let Honey sniff her and lick her hands.

"You're so pretty, yes you are. Aren't you a good dog?" Isabella whispered, smoothing her hand over the velvet fur on the top of Honey's head. Honey closed her eyes blissfully and leaned against Isabella, breathing in the sunny smells of outdoors.

"I shouldn't be doing this, but I can't not love you, can I?" Isabella sighed. "Not when you're so sweet. But we have to pretend when Sam's around, okay?"

Honey could hear the sadness in Isabella's voice, and she leaned harder against her legs, rubbing her muzzle against Isabella's knee.

"Yes, you're a good girl— Oh!"

Honey sprang up, hearing the crunch of gravel, and barked excitedly. Now Sam was back, too, and she had both of them. Sam was her first person, her best friend, but she adored Isabella, too, and she loved it when they both played with her.

As the key clicked in the lock, Isabella jumped up. Honey glanced around nervously. What was wrong?

All of a sudden, she remembered that angry, frightening moment in the kitchen the day before, and she let out a tiny whine as the door opened. She tried to wiggle back behind Isabella's legs to be safe, but Isabella pushed her away.

Honey stood uncertainly in the middle of the hallway, not liking this strange feeling at all. She tucked her tail between her legs and stared up at Sam, her ears flattened with worry.

"Isabella...."

Isabella looked up as Sam stuck his head around her bedroom door. She had hurried away from Honey as soon

as she heard him coming home, but
she wasn't sure she'd gotten away with
it. She had a feeling it was obvious that
she'd been fussing over the puppy.

"Yes?" she asked, trying not to sound
guilty.

"Look, I'm sorry."

Isabella's eyes widened, and then she
couldn't help smiling as Honey nosed
around Sam's legs and pushed the door
open wider.

"Wow, she got up the stairs fast,"
Sam muttered. "She couldn't manage
them at all when we first got her. Hey,
careful." He caught hold of Honey's
collar. "No chewing Isabella's stuff."

Isabella looked around her room.
Honey didn't come upstairs very often,
and she hadn't puppy-proofed it.

There *were* quite a lot of things on the floor....

"Can I sit down?" Sam asked, and Isabella nodded. She was still confused by this suddenly friendly Sam. She eyed him cautiously as he sat on the floor and pulled Honey into his lap.

"Does she want this?" Isabella asked shyly, holding out a scrunched-up ball of paper.

"Oh, yeah, excellent." Sam reached for it and offered it to Honey, who eyed the paper with tiny growls. "It's going to end up shredded all over your floor, though."

"That's okay."

They sat in embarrassed silence for a moment, while Honey growled and scratched at the paper ball. Then Sam sighed. "So, I talked to my dad. He noticed that I was upset yesterday. I shouldn't have said those things."

Isabella opened and shut her mouth, and eventually just shrugged. She didn't know what to say.

"I know you weren't really trying to take Honey from me. I was kind of worried about something else…."

Did you know I'm going to stay with my
mom when summer vacation starts?"

Isabella looked thoughtful. "I think
my mom said something about it."

"Yeah, for two weeks. Which is a
long time. I mean, I want to see her,
but the thing is, I can't take Honey."
Sam ducked his head to rub his cheek
against the puppy's ears.

"Oh, that's a long time. Um…. Why can't you take her?"

"Because my mom's apartment is tiny, and there's no yard. It's right in the middle of town, too. It's so busy around there. And my dad's taking me on the train. Honey wouldn't like that, either." He sighed and hugged Honey tighter. "Anyway … I'm going to have to leave Honey here. So … you can see why I was upset. But actually—" Sam took a deep breath—"actually it's a good thing Honey likes you because it means you can help Dad take care of her. He's promised to make a big fuss over her so she doesn't feel like she's been abandoned, but he's always so busy with work."

"I'll help," Isabella said eagerly. She

got up and came to sit next to him, leaning against her bed. "I'd love to. And I can see why you said that stuff. I do know Honey's your dog … I'd never try to make her mine. I can show her photos of you, or something…."

Sam snorted. "She'd probably just eat them!" But he sounded a little happier, Isabella thought, and Honey seemed to think so, too—she was looking lovingly up at Sam and beating her tail against his leg.

Chapter Four
Missing Sam

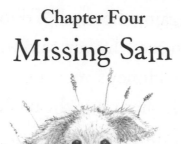

Honey stuck her nose curiously into the bag and sniffed around. It smelled like Sam. She wondered what he was doing, squashing all of his things inside—a couple of pairs of shoes, a tattered book. She could smell food, too—a packet of something sweet and delicious. She put her paws up on the side of the bag so she could get farther in and sniff everything properly.

Then she squeaked in surprise as something soft landed on top of her and everything went dark. Crossly, she wriggled out from underneath it, shaking her ears and looking around to see what had happened.

"Oops, I'm sorry, Honey." Sam picked up the hoodie he'd thrown on top of the bag, looking guilty. "I didn't see you. Are you okay?" He crouched down and rubbed the puppy's head. "You can't get in there. I wish you could come with me, but you wouldn't like it." He sighed.

Honey wasn't sure what was going on, but Sam's voice sounded worried and sad. She edged around the bag and tried to climb into his lap to snuggle up with him.

"Are you trying to cheer me up?" Sam sniffed, and then laughed as Honey shoved her nose in his ear. "It's all right, Honey. I'm looking forward to seeing Mom. And Dad and Isabella have promised to take good care of you."

Honey looked around as Mike shouted from downstairs. "Sam! Are you almost ready? Come on. We have to head for the station soon."

Sam gave her a hug. "Bye, Honey. See you soon."

Honey followed Sam to the door, getting under his feet as he struggled with the big bag. She went cautiously down the stairs after him, hopping from step to step. She was better at getting up

the stairs, but somehow, they seemed
a lot steeper on the way down. When
she arrived at the bottom, everyone in
the house was there. Isabella and her
mom were hugging Sam, and Mike
was taking Sam's bag out to the car.
Honey stood watching them, her ears
twitching worriedly. Sam was going
somewhere…. She stumbled down the
last step, ready to dart after him.

"Hey, Honey, you stay here," Isabella said, coming to sit next to her. "No dashing out the front door."

Honey gave Isabella's hand a quick lick, but she was still watching Sam. There was something wrong—she could feel it. Sam left the house all of the time, but this seemed different. She didn't trust that big bag, and she whined anxiously as Sam went to the door. He looked at her and waved, and then he shut the door behind him.

What was happening? Honey howled—a long, frightened wail.

Isabella had been looking forward to fussing over Honey and giving her tons of love and attention while Sam was away. She'd been confident she could stop the little dog from missing Sam, but it turned out to be much harder than she'd thought. Every so often, Honey would stop and look around for him, as though she thought he was only in the next room. If anyone mentioned his name, she'd get really excited and run to the door. Isabella got very good at making up silly chase games with Honey's toys to distract her.

During the week, she and Mike went on long walks with Honey, early in the morning before it got too hot. Mom came, too, when she wasn't at work. They usually went to the park, but they did go back to Sam's favorite woods once to splash in the stream.

Mike showed Isabella how to make a dam out of sticks and mud, so that the tiny stream built up into a pool. They had to take it apart before they went home again, but Honey loved having her own little paddling pool. She kept putting her nose under the water, and then she would pop up with a confused look and make huge snorting noises. Then she shook herself dry all over Isabella and Mike.

The first weekend Sam was away,

Mom and Mike took Isabella and Beatrice to a country show that was being held in a big field just outside the town. The girls had been looking forward to it for a long time, especially as dogs were allowed so Honey could come, too. There were farm animals to look at, as well as stalls and displays and a competition tent with cakes and jams and things people had made. Isabella had entered Best Potato Person, with a fluffy-eared potato dog that looked like Honey. When they walked around the tent to look at everything, she found a ribbon on it saying second prize.

"You should have won first!" Beatrice said, eyeing the potato fairy that had come in first. "Yours is much better."

"Can you pose next to it with Honey, Isabella?" Mike suggested, taking out his phone. "We can send the photo to Sam."

Isabella nodded happily, but then she saw that Honey's head was up. The puppy was looking around eagerly, her tail wagging and her eyes bright. She'd heard Mike say Sam's name, and she thought he was coming. It was hard to smile for the photo when Honey looked so lost.

"Not much longer," she whispered to Honey as they wandered through the fair. "One more week, and he'll be home."

"Oh, there's a dog show!" Beatrice pointed at a sign by the big show-ring. "You could enter Honey! I bet she'd win waggiest tail!"

Isabella looked down at the puppy, frowning. "I don't think she would at the moment...." Honey wasn't wagging her tail at all. Her head was drooping, and Isabella had never seen her look so sad.

Beatrice crouched on the grass next to the puppy. "Poor Honey.... Do you think all the people are scaring her?"

Isabella ran her hand gently along Honey's back. "No. I think she's missing—" She turned her head away from the puppy and dropped her voice to a whisper—"Sam. She heard Mike say his name."

"Oh, Honey…," Beatrice said quietly. "Isn't there any way we can cheer her up?"

"I can't think of anything," Isabella said gloomily. "I'd buy her a hot dog with my allowance if that would make her feel better, but she just walked past a whole pile of chips someone dropped without even looking. Usually she'd be trying to gobble them all up." She made a face at Beatrice. "It's another whole week until he's back. That's a long time for a puppy to be miserable."

"Maybe he could talk to her on the phone?" Beatrice suggested.

Isabella looked thoughtful. "Yes, I bet she'd recognize his voice. Oh! Even better! He could video call her! Then she'd be able to see him as well. You'd love that, Honey, wouldn't you?" Isabella crouched down to give the mournful puppy a hug.

Honey lifted her paw and scratched at Sam's bedroom door again. She had tried looking for him in his room before, and he hadn't been there, but he had to be *somewhere*. Mike had been talking about him when they'd been out—she'd heard him say Sam's name.

That must mean Sam was close by!

"He's not there, Honey. But we're going to make sure you can see him soon."

Isabella had followed her upstairs. Honey glanced at her and then back at the door. Her tail drooped. She couldn't hear anyone in the room. It was quiet. Empty.

"Come on, sweetheart. Come and watch TV with me." Isabella's voice was coaxing, and Honey padded toward her, twitching her tail just a little. Isabella was warm, and gentle, and very good at scratching ears, even if it wasn't quite the same as being with Sam.

"Should I pick you up?" Isabella suggested, hesitating at the top of the stairs. "You don't like going down, do you?" She scooped Honey into her arms, and the puppy nuzzled gratefully under her chin as they headed downstairs to the living room.

"What should we watch?" Isabella said, curling up at one end of the couch with Honey in her lap. "A movie?"

She turned on the TV and pulled a blanket around both of them. Some of the strange unhappiness inside Honey eased as Isabella petted her, running the fur of Honey's ears between her fingers. The puppy's breathing slowed to a soft wheeze, and her eyelids fluttered closed. Her head slumped heavily on Isabella's arm, and Honey slept.

Chapter Five
Missing!

"I have to get back in a minute," Isabella said. She sat up on the bench in the yard and peered through Beatrice's kitchen window—she could just see the clock. "Sam's going to video call Mike at twelve so he can talk to Honey."

"Oh, wonderful!" Beatrice nodded excitedly. "She'll love it. It was so sad seeing how much she missed him the other day."

"I know." Isabella smiled. "I can't wait to see Honey when she realizes it's Sam on the screen! And then it's only a few days until he's back for real." She glanced at the clock again. "Actually, I'd better go now. Sam might call early. Mike said he was really excited about it. He's missed Honey a lot, too!"

"Yeah, see you! Let me know how it goes."

Isabella opened the gate with a wave. "I'll shout for you later," she called back. All the houses along the street were built with a side path that went around to the backyard, so all she had to do was slip out of Beatrice's

gate and through hers. Isabella banged
the gate behind her and hurried into
the house.

"Honey! Hey, Honey, look."

Honey blinked sleepily at Isabella
from her basket, where she'd been
napping.

"It's Sam, Honey. Come and see
him!"

Honey leaped up out of the basket,
looking around eagerly. Sam! Where
was he? Why couldn't she see him?

She plodded back over to her
basket, her head hanging, and curled
up again, with her nose buried in the
cushion. Sam wasn't there, and Honey

was starting to wonder if he was ever coming back.

"Aww, she looks so sad. I wasn't sure if she'd actually miss me."

Honey put her head up, puzzled but almost hopeful. That was Sam's voice. It was different—crackly and faraway—but it was definitely him! She stood up in the basket, gazing around cautiously. If Sam were here, why couldn't she see him or smell him? Why wasn't he down on the floor hugging her? Everyone else was in the kitchen, Mike and Isabella and Isabella's mom, but she still couldn't see Sam.

"I don't think she's figured it out yet," Isabella said, looking at something on the table. "Here, I'll move the laptop so she can see you."

Honey looked on, confused, as Isabella moved something on to the floor in front of her, and then came to sit beside her. "Can you see him, Honey? It's Sam!"

"Honey! Hey!"

It was Sam's voice again, but Honey still couldn't find him. There was a strange blurry thing moving on the screen that looked a little like Sam. She didn't like it. Honey backed away uncertainly. It scared her. The screen smelled sharp and unpleasant, and the shape flickered and jerked. She whined and kept backing up until she bumped into her basket and made herself jump. She let out an unhappy growl and shot across the kitchen to the open back door. She had to get away.

"Oh, no, I don't think Honey understood what was happening," Mike said. "I guess she's never seen you on a screen. It must have been weird for her. Don't worry, Sam; we'll go and find her and cheer her up. I can throw her ball for her since she's in the yard."

"I thought she'd like it," Sam said miserably. "I really miss her."

"She misses you, too," Isabella said.

"If we say your name, she looks for you."

"But Isabella's doing an amazing job taking care of her," Mike said. "We've been going on a lot of walks."

"And you'll be back in a few days," Isabella's mom put in comfortingly. "She'll see you soon."

"I guess," Sam said, sighing. "Can you go and find her, Dad? Make sure she's okay. She looked so confused."

"Of course. See you soon, Sam. Get your mom to text me which train you're catching on the way back, all right? Bye!" Mike ended the call and closed the laptop. "Let's go and find Honey. She looked really spooked, poor little thing."

Isabella hurried out into the yard.

She was expecting to see Honey flopped underneath the table on the patio—the puppy liked the shade in the hot summer weather—but she wasn't there. Maybe she was hiding under one of the bushes.

"Honey!" Isabella called, looking around the yard.

"You can't see her?" Mike asked, standing in the kitchen doorway. "She probably went right to the end." He started to walk down the long strip of grass, shouting for Honey.

He and Isabella both turned hopefully when they heard a scuffling sound. But it was just Beatrice, peering over from next door. There was a bench up against the fence on the other side, and Beatrice was standing on it.

"Did Honey like seeing Sam?" she asked.

Isabella shook her head. "She hated it. I wish I'd never suggested it. I don't think she knew what was happening, and she looked so confused. And then she ran out into the yard to get away.

So we've come out to play with her and cheer her up. You could come and help, if you like. Mike, can Beatrice come over?"

Mike came walking back up the yard. "Yes, sure. I haven't found Honey yet, though. She must be tucked away somewhere, hiding. I didn't realize the video call would upset her so much."

"I'll just ask my mom," Beatrice called over the fence. "I can come around by the side gate." She disappeared back into her own yard, shouting for her mom.

"I'll make sure it's not locked," Mike said, starting toward the gate, and then he stopped, looking worried. "Hang on, it's open!"

"What?" Isabella rushed along the patio to look. Mike was right— the gate was standing open, and she could see all the way up the path to the front of the house. "But Honey...."

"Don't panic," Mike said, but Isabella thought he sounded as if he were panicking a bit. "It doesn't mean she went out there. She could still be hiding somewhere in the yard."

"But she isn't," Isabella said. "You looked everywhere. We called. She comes when we call. She isn't there."

Beatrice appeared at the gate, beaming at them, but then her smile faded. "What's the matter?"

"The gate…. The gate was open!" Isabella cried, darting past her friend and up the path to the front of the house. Her heart was thumping, and she felt cold all over. What if Honey had run out into the street? There was no fence along the front of the house, just a gravel driveway. That was why everyone was so careful about not letting Honey dash out of the front door. "Honey!" she called. "Honey, where are you?"

"Honey!" Mike and Beatrice had

come up the path behind her, and
Mike was kneeling down to check if
the puppy was hiding under the car.
"Not there." He hurried out to the
pavement and looked up and down
the street. "I can't see any sign of her.
Maybe I'll go and check the backyard
again. We'd feel silly if we went
searching for her and she was hiding
behind the shed the whole time."

Isabella looked at Mike, her eyes
wide with horror. "I think I let her out.
I ran around the side of the house from
Beatrice's, because I wanted to be back
when Sam called. I must not have shut
the gate all the way. I didn't stop to
check that the latch clicked. You said
always make sure it clicks!"

"It's okay, Isabella, don't worry."

Mike chewed his bottom lip. "It was an accident. Just one of those things. The gate didn't catch. It doesn't sometimes. Hey, don't cry! No one's upset with you. It's all right."

"It's not all right," Isabella gulped. "Sam wanted me to take care of Honey, and now she's run away, and it's all because of me!"

Chapter Six
Looking for Honey

Honey pressed herself against a
garden wall as a car rushed past. She
wasn't scared of cars when she was
out with Sam or Isabella or Mike, but
everything felt so different now that
she was all on her own.

She looked back up the street. She
could just see the house, and for a
moment, she thought about going

home. Then she shivered. She knew she couldn't bear to see that strange trembling picture again. *That* wasn't Sam.

Where was he, though? She had definitely heard him. He'd said her name! She knew he wasn't in the house, but she was sure he must be somewhere close by.

Honey put her nose down and sniffed, looking for any traces. The fences and walls and lampposts she'd passed were covered in layers of smells, and Honey loved to investigate them whenever they went out. She could pick out her own scent from all of their walks, as well as other dogs and Isabella—and, yes, there was Sam's scent, too, but it was old and stale.

What should she do? Hearing Sam's
voice had made her miss him more
than ever. She wanted him to be sitting
on the living-room floor so she could
flop over his legs while he played
video games. She loved to snooze like
that, just opening one eye when he
shouted at the screen. Honey whined,
remembering. She wanted to be with
Sam so much.

She sniffed again and caught a faint

scent of leaves and damp earth. Her tail twitched into a wag.

The woods!

"Any luck?" Isabella's mom asked anxiously as Isabella and Beatrice ran along the street toward her.

"No." Isabella's voice shook as she answered. She still couldn't believe she'd left the gate open. How could she have been so careless?

Mike came hurrying up. He'd been checking down at the other end of the street, toward the park, while the girls knocked on the neighbors' doors and Mom checked the street. "Did you go all the way to the corner?"

Mom nodded. "I kept on calling for her. I suppose she could have gone farther," she said doubtfully. "It hasn't been all that long, though. She hasn't been gone more than, what, half an hour?"

Mike ran a hand through his hair and sighed. "I just don't know where to look. There are so many places she could be hiding. I keep checking my phone, hoping someone's found her and they'll call the number on her collar."

"We'd better get you back home, Beatrice," Mom said, looking at her watch. "It'll be your lunchtime."

"It's all right. Mom won't mind," Beatrice started to say, but then she spotted her mom standing on her front door step, waving to them.

"Did you go for a walk?" she called, looking puzzled.

"It's Honey," Mike explained. "We were out looking for her. She slipped out of the backyard."

Isabella stood half behind her mom. She couldn't bear to explain to anyone else that she had been the one who'd left the gate open.

"Oh, no…. Why don't you put a message on the online neighborhood group?" Beatrice's mom suggested. "Someone down the street did that when their cat disappeared a couple of weeks ago, do you remember? It turned out that he was shut in a garage."

"Good idea. I'll do that now," Mike said, reaching for his phone. He smiled at Isabella and Mom. "Why don't you grab some lunch? I'm going to keep looking for a little longer."

"I'll come back and continue looking after lunch. I can, can't I, Mom?" Beatrice asked.

Her mom nodded. "Of course. Don't look so worried, Isabella. I'm sure you'll find Honey soon."

But even though they kept on
searching all afternoon, there was
no sign of the puppy. None of the
neighbors had seen her, either—she
seemed to have disappeared completely.
Mom had to go to work after a while,
and Beatrice could only help for an
hour after lunch, then she had to go
and see her grandma, but Mike and
Isabella walked for hours. They went
all around the streets, peering under
cars and into front yards, calling
Honey's name over and over again.

They were heading back along their
own street when Mike's phone beeped,
and Isabella looked up hopefully.

Mike shook his head. "Just someone

promising to let us know if they see her." He sighed. "Come on. Let's go and have some dinner, okay? I know you probably don't feel like it, but I bet you didn't eat much lunch."

"Neither did you. Mom made you a sandwich, and you didn't even stop to eat it." Isabella sniffed. "What are we going to tell Sam?" She'd been thinking about that all afternoon in between worrying about Honey.

Mike put his arm around her. "Hopefully we're not going to have to tell him anything. She hasn't been missing that long, Isabella. Although if we don't find her by tomorrow, then yes, I'll have to call him." He crouched down to look her in the eye. "Honestly, Isabella love, it's not your fault. I should have put a new latch on the gate. Please don't be upset about it."

"I don't want to stop looking," Isabella whispered.

"I know, but we've been walking for hours, Isabella. You look exhausted— you're practically falling over your feet. We can heat up some of that lasagna I made yesterday."

"I could make some posters while you're doing that," Isabella suggested. "Mom lets me use her laptop."

"Good idea! We can put them up in the morning if we still haven't found her."

Back at the house, Isabella found Mom's laptop in the living room and opened it up. Mom had a file of photos, and there were some good pictures of Honey. Isabella chose one where she was looking particularly fluffy and cute. People would make more effort to keep an eye out for Honey if they could see how little and sweet she was, wouldn't they? She typed LOST across the top of the page and swallowed hard. How could she have been so careless?

Isabella added a description of Honey, and then Mike's phone number and Mom's, too. Then she wrote *Please help us find her!* She printed ten copies,

just to start with, and went back into
the kitchen to show them to Mike.

"Let's see." Mike sighed as he
admired the photo of Honey. "I'm sorry,
Isabella. It's great … for a moment, I'd
forgotten how little she is."

"I know," Isabella said, her voice very
small.

Mike smiled at her. "Come on. Let's
have some food."

Isabella was tired—almost too tired
to eat. She kept stabbing her fork into
the lasagna and pushing pieces around.
Then she looked at the food going cold
on her plate and thought sadly that
Honey would probably love it. The

puppy wouldn't have had anything to
eat since that morning. She must be so
hungry. Eventually, Isabella managed
to swallow a few mouthfuls, and then
she looked up at Mike.

"Yeah, I'm not feeling hungry either.
Ready to go back out? I thought we
could try the park again. There's always
a bunch of dogs being walked around
this time of the evening. Maybe she
wanted to find some friends."

Isabella nodded, but she could tell that Mike was forcing himself to sound cheerful. They didn't really have any idea where Honey might have gone.

"Do you think she could find her way home?" she asked as they headed down the street toward the park. "Dogs are supposed to be good at that."

"I don't know. I hope so, but she's only a puppy...."

They were both silent after that, walking and watching, and every so often calling for Honey. That afternoon, they'd been shouting her name eagerly every few seconds, as if they expected her to leap out and come dashing over to them. Now when they called, neither of them sounded very hopeful.

At last Mike said, "I think we need

to head back, Isabella. I know it's not dark yet, but it's almost eight."

"But Honey…," Isabella protested. How could they leave her out all night?

"I know." Mike sighed. "I just don't think we're doing any good right now. We'd be better off getting some sleep and having more energy to look for her in the morning. Maybe you and Beatrice can put those posters up."

The posters that she'd been hoping they wouldn't have to use, Isabella thought miserably. She trailed after Mike back to the house. She hated how quiet it was when they opened the front door. No Honey rushing to greet them, squeaking and snuffling and trying to lick them all over. The house seemed so empty without her.

Chapter Seven
In the Woods

Honey was tracking along a narrow
pathway—one that she thought she
remembered from walks with Sam.
It had a high, earthy bank all along
one side, riddled with interesting little
holes. If she hadn't been so desperate
to find Sam, she would have stopped
and tried to dig…. But she had more
important things to think about. She

had been out here a long time now. Sam would be wondering where she was, and so would Isabella. She'd seen a few people—several of them had stopped to pet her. One man had tried to catch her collar, but she'd darted away into the trees, and he'd sighed and continued with his walk.

She shook her ears briskly and trotted on, snuffling every so often at piles of leaves or fallen branches for Sam's scent. She was so busy sniffing at a tall clump of grass by the side of the path that she didn't see a plump, gray squirrel dashing down a tree trunk. The squirrel raced across the path in front of her and then pulled up short, staring at her in horror.

Honey froze, unsure what she was supposed to do. She'd never seen a squirrel so close up—she could see it breathing, its tiny chest heaving in and out. The squirrel seemed as shocked as she was. It chittered furiously at her for a moment and then shot away up a tree on the other side of the path, leaving Honey staring after it.

After the squirrel disappeared,

Honey looked around a little
anxiously. The bright summer light
was fading now, and the trees were
full of noises—chirrups and rustling
and the hiss of the wind through
the leaves. She hadn't even noticed
that squirrel. What else was out here,
watching her? Honey shivered, and
the fur around her neck prickled, and
she stood up.

Isabella had been so tired when they got back to the house that she'd had to drag herself up the stairs, but once she was in bed, she just didn't feel like sleeping. She couldn't seem to find a comfortable way to lie, and her bed was too hot. In the end she sat up, leaning against her pillow with her arms wrapped around her knees. She couldn't stop thinking about Honey, out there on her own. She must be so scared. Then there was Sam. He didn't even know that Honey was missing, but he was going to get a phone call from his dad in the morning....

And she was supposed to go to sleep! Isabella got out of bed and pulled on the clothes she'd been wearing earlier and a hoodie, because it was cooler now. It was still light outside. Mike would be downstairs, waiting for Mom to get home from work. They could go up and down their street one last time. Mike had only stopped them from searching because he thought she was tired. What if Honey had been scared and was hiding somewhere? Now that most people had gone home and it was quieter, she might decide to come back out. They couldn't miss her!

Isabella hurried downstairs to talk to Mike, but when she went into the living room, she saw that he was fast asleep on the couch, snoring faintly. She stood in the doorway, wondering what to do. She started forward, meaning to wake him, but then she couldn't bring herself to do it.

It was my fault, so I should handle this, she thought. *I could go and put those posters up at the same time.... Mom wouldn't mind that. I'm only going down the street.*

Actually, Isabella was pretty sure that Mom *would* mind, but she was too worried about Honey to think about that. She slipped out of the house through the back door. That meant going through the side gate, which made her eyes fill with tears. Isabella stopped for a moment, blinking hard and looking at Beatrice's gate. Maybe Beatrice could come with her to put up the posters. No. She shook her head—it was too late. Beatrice's mom wouldn't let her go out now.

Just like mine wouldn't.... Isabella hurried guiltily up the side path and flitted along the street, taping the posters to lampposts. She'd stuck up almost all of them when she came to the little alley that led to the woods. She stopped in her tracks.

The woods! They hadn't searched there!

Mike almost always walked Honey in the park, Isabella realized. Obviously, he hadn't thought of the little path to Pine Grove when they'd been searching, and she hadn't, either. She tucked the sticky tape and the leftover posters into her hoodie pockets and started down the alley.

It wasn't dark yet, but the high fences shut out some of the light, and Isabella found herself half running toward the woods, although she knew it would be darker in among the trees. *I don't care,* she told herself firmly. *I bet Honey's scared on her own in the dark, too. I'm going to find her.* She felt almost certain now. How could they have forgotten to search the woods? Honey loved them, and so did Sam. Of course she would run to the woods if she were upset or frightened. If she were looking for Sam….

The tall grass in the clearing looked dry and limp as Isabella crossed it, but the woods still had that cool smell of damp new growth. Isabella pulled her hoodie around her more tightly and plunged into the dimness under the trees.

It was getting darker, and there was still no sign of Sam. Honey thought that she must be getting close to the stream, but it was hard to remember

all of the twisting paths. Should she
continue looking for him down by the
water? She padded on, sniffing for
the fresh smell of the stream, but she
couldn't catch it on the air. Maybe it
wasn't this way after all…. She whined
uncertainly. The woods felt bigger
without Sam or Isabella, and darker.

A loud growling behind her on
the path sent Honey into a sudden
frightened crouch, huddling against
the earthy bank. Was it another dog?
Why did it sound so angry?

There was an answering shout—
"No, Bertie. No! Leave the squirrel
alone!"—followed by more growling,
and a fierce scratching and scuffling of
paws.

Honey looked frantically back and

forth, wondering what to do. She didn't want to be anywhere near that dog, or the woman shouting. She scurried along the path, but she could still hear the woman talking crossly to the dog. "What have you found now? No more chasing squirrels, Bertie."

Honey felt the woods grow quiet. She could *hear* the other dog listening. She felt the curious silence, and then suddenly, there were heavy paws thumping along the path and deep, eager breathing.

The other dog was following her.

Honey sped up, and then she spotted a dark hollow in the bank, where the roots of a great tree had come creeping down. The earth had been washed away by years of rain,

leaving a hole just
big enough for a
frightened little
dog. Honey
tucked
herself
inside,
trying not
to sneeze as
loose earth rained
down around her ears.
Where was Sam? Where was
Isabella? Honey watched, mouse-quiet,
as the dog came stomping closer.

Chapter Eight
Safe at Last

Isabella hadn't thought about other people being in the woods, but she supposed it was a popular place for an evening walk, especially after such a hot a day. She almost asked a woman pulling a huge dog if she'd seen Honey, but then she thought that she'd better not. For starters, the woman and the dog both looked grumpy, and Mom wouldn't want her talking to strangers anyway. The woman with the dog would probably be shocked that Isabella was out alone this late, too. She might think Isabella was lost and she should take her home. Isabella slipped off the path and ducked behind a huge, scraggly bush, waiting for them to walk past.

"No more chasing things, Bertie! I think that was a rabbit, poor little thing. You're a great big monster. Come on, let's go home!"

Isabella watched them stomp by. She shivered as the silence settled over the woods again. She wasn't lost, not exactly, but it was weird how different the paths looked in the dim evening light. When the woman with

the dog was gone, Isabella came back
out onto the path and looked around
uncertainly. It was getting colder. And
the shadows were deeper. She found
that she was clutching tightly at her
arms and gave herself a shake.

"Stop it," she muttered out loud.
"You're supposed to be looking for
Honey." She marched along the path.
She couldn't get lost if she stuck to
this same one, could she? "Honey!" she
called, trying hard to keep her voice
from wobbling. "Here, girl! Honey!"
But no matter how loud she tried to
shout, her voice sounded thin and faint
in the old woods. The trees seemed
to be pressing closer in on the path,
growing taller and darker, and Isabella's
voice shivered away.

Something chattered sharply in the trees above her, and Isabella whirled around, squeaking with fright. What was it? There was a scurrying, like little claws, and she saw a squirrel race along a branch.

Just a squirrel! It was silly to be scared of such a tiny creature, but she couldn't help it. Her heart felt as if it were swinging around inside her, and she was cold all over.

Another scuffling noise farther up the path—something down on the ground this time—made her press her hands against her mouth. She imagined a fox, or maybe a huge fierce dog, or even a wolf—although she knew that that was silly. Isabella almost shut her eyes so she didn't have to see what it was, but what good would that do? Whatever it was would just be able to eat her more easily…. She clenched her fingernails tightly into her palms and forced herself to look.

Wriggling out from under a knot of tree roots at the foot of the bank was a dusty, scruffy, golden dog.

"Honey!" Isabella yelped, crouching down and opening her arms—and Honey shot into them, trembling and whining.

Honey nestled against Isabella's shoulder, pressing her nose into the place between Isabella's chin and her neck. She could smell that Isabella had

been scared, too,
but everything
was all right
now—they were
together.

Isabella might
not be Sam, but
she was kind,
and she scratched
ears well, and she
smelled like home.

"We've been looking for you all day,"
Isabella was saying as she stumbled
back up the path with Honey in her
arms. "Have you been out here in the
woods all this time? We should have
looked here earlier."

Honey felt Isabella's heart thump
a little harder as they came into the

narrow alley that led back to the
street and she nuzzled close, swiping
Isabella's chin with her tongue and
making her giggle.

"It's okay," Isabella said. "The alley
isn't very long. It just feels a little spooky.
There!" She sighed. "Back on our street
now." She was silent for a moment as
they hurried along, and then she added,
"I wonder if Mike woke up…. I guess
even if he did, he wouldn't know that I
went out. Maybe we can tell him and
Mom tomorrow. I don't know."

Honey snuffled in Isabella's ear. She
didn't understand what Isabella was
saying, but Isabella sounded anxious.

"No, we can't do that," Isabella said.
"It would be mean. I don't want Mike
going to bed thinking you're still lost.

Or Mom. I bet she's been worrying about you all the way through her shift. We can't not tell them—that's silly."

As they reached the house, Honey tensed and then struggled in Isabella's arms, remembering the strange version of Sam she'd seen earlier.

"Hey, careful!" Isabella stopped, looking down at Honey worriedly. "What is it? Oh…. I bet you're still upset about that video call." She swallowed. "He's not here, Honey. But he's coming home in a few days, I promise. Not long to wait." She crouched down and put Honey on the gravel, keeping hold of her collar, and Honey eyed the house doubtfully.

"I don't want to take you inside, not if you're scared," Isabella whispered.

"What should we do, Honey?"

Honey tugged uncertainly at Isabella holding her collar. She didn't quite know what she wanted. Not to go back to the woods, she was sure of that. She had spent a long time huddling under those roots until the other dog had left, frightened by every noise and breath of wind. When she'd seen Isabella on the path, she'd been so grateful, so relieved.

Isabella wasn't going to let anything hurt her, Honey decided. She tugged again, pulling Isabella toward the house, and saw her smile.

"Let's go around the side and in the back door. I don't want to wake up Mike by ringing the bell...."

When they got there, Isabella pushed the door open, and they both peered into the kitchen cautiously. As soon as Honey saw her food bowl, she remembered how hungry she was. She pulled herself out of Isabella's grip and dashed to stand by it, looking up at Isabella hopefully.

"I forgot you must be starving!
Here."

Honey watched, tail wagging, as
Isabella pulled out the food bag from
the cupboard and filled her bowl, then
rinsed out and refilled her water bowl,
too. Honey ate greedily, gulping down
her food to ease the aching hunger
inside her.

"Good girl," Isabella told her. "Oh, I
just had an idea! Stay there a minute."

Honey didn't even notice her darting
out of the kitchen. She gobbled up
every scrap of her late dinner and
slumped wearily onto the floor by her
bowl. Then she glanced around at last,
surprised to see that Isabella was gone.
She stood up again uncertainly, all of
the strangeness rushing back.

"It's okay! It's okay, Honey, look."
Isabella hurried back in. "Were you
scared? Look, I brought you this." She
crouched down by Honey's basket,
laying something inside.

Honey padded over cautiously to see
what it was. She sniffed at the faded
old sweatshirt, and then sniffed again
in delight when she recognized the
smell.

"It's the one Sam wears as a pajama
top sometimes," Isabella explained,
arranging it in a ball at the side of
Honey's basket. "I'm sure it has to
smell like him. Is that nice? I went
upstairs to get it, and I wanted to see
where Mike was. He's still asleep on
the couch, Honey! So I left a note on
the coffee table. Mom's going to be so

upset with me in the morning, but I got you back, so maybe she'll go easy on me. Night night, Honey."

Isabella ran one hand gently down the puppy's back, and Honey shivered with pleasure. She was home and full and sleepy, and she had Sam's shirt. She watched, her nose resting on the edge of the basket, as Isabella tiptoed out of the kitchen.

She could hear her going quietly up the stairs. If she listened carefully enough, she could hear Mike faintly snoring in the living room.

Honey shook herself and stood up. She didn't want to be alone. She stumbled out of her basket, dragging the sweatshirt with her, and set off through the kitchen and up the stairs. At last, she clambered exhaustedly onto the landing and padded into Isabella's room.

"Hey! What is it?" Isabella whispered as Honey scrambled up onto the bed. "Did you come to find me?" She giggled. "And you brought Sam's sweatshirt."

The puppy stretched out next to Isabella, the sweatshirt bunched between her paws. She was home and safe....

"So what did Dad say the next morning?" Sam asked as they headed along the path through the woods for their first walk since he got back home. He was smirking, and Isabella shrugged.

"Nothing. I think he was a little embarrassed that he slept through my sneaking out *and* back in again." She sighed. "My mom had a lot to say, though. She made me promise that I'd never, ever go out on my own ever, ever, ever again. And she wouldn't let me go over to Beatrice's. I'm surprised she's letting me go out with you. Look, that's where Honey was, tucked under those roots."

"Wow…." Sam crouched down to look and watched Honey sniffing at the hole cautiously. "She remembers, I bet. Look at her. It's okay, Honey. I'm not going away again for a long time, I promise." He smiled at Isabella. "Thanks for taking care of her."

"I let her get out!" Isabella stared at him. "And it was my fault that she was so upset in the first place. I looked it up on Mom's laptop—some dogs really don't like seeing people they know on screens because they don't see the same way we do. You must have looked really strange to her."

"Yeah, maybe. But you were trying to cheer her up. And when she ran away, you got her back again. You didn't give up."

"I suppose...." Isabella leaned down to pet Honey, and the little dog stopped investigating the hole under the roots and put her front paws up on Isabella's knees, panting happily. "I was so scared. It made it even worse that she's your puppy, and I'd lost her. I had to find you, didn't I?" She rubbed Honey's ears and laughed as the puppy licked her nose.

"She's your puppy, too," Sam said, and Isabella smiled at him.

There in the dappled sun under the trees, with Honey scratching lovingly at her shorts, Isabella thought that maybe he was right.